Houdini and the Five-Cent Circus

KEITH GRAY

HOUDINI AND THE FIVE-CENT CIRCUS

Barrington Stoke

For Clara and Jasmine

First published in 2018 in Great Britain by
Barrington Stoke Ltd
18 Walker Street, Edinburgh, EH3 7LP

www.barringtonstoke.co.uk

A CIP catalogue record for this book is available from the British Library upon request

ISBN: 978-1-78112-810-7

Printed in China by Leo

CONTENTS

1.	The Dare	1
2.	The Unlocked Doors	9
3.	The Sheriff's Handcuffs	21
4.	The Two Tickets	40
5.	The English Magician	53
6.	The Overheard Conversation	62
7.	The Twins	69
8.	The Kiss	79
9.	The First Escape	89
10.	The Five-Cent Circus	92

Inspired by true events from the childhood of Harry Houdini

"What the eyes see and the ears hear, the mind believes."

HARRY HOUDINI

CHAPTER 1

The Dare

Erik had vanished.

"Where is he?" Jack asked. His teeth chattered louder than a shook-up bag of marbles. Maybe because he was freezing cold, or maybe because he was nervous. Probably both. "Can you see him?" Jack continued. "He can't have just disappeared."

"Maybe he's got himself caught already," I said.

We were both worried. It was close to midnight. We were hunkered in the shadows of a big oak tree on the corner of College Avenue and Superior Street. We leaned around the tree trunk to peer along College Avenue, hoping to spot Erik. But there was no one to be seen.

"You're the one who dared Erik to do this," I said to Jack. "It's your fault if he's got caught."

"How was I to know he'd really do it?" Jack snapped back.

"You shouldn't dare Erik to do anything," I said. "Not ever."

It was late October in the year 1885, and the sidewalks in Appleton were crunchy with leaves. It was real cold that year. So cold that the lumps of horse-dung were rock hard, and you could play kick-and-run with them in the street. So cold it could freeze the boogers up your nose. Which wasn't my most lady-like of thoughts, but the older I got the more I realised being lady-like and speaking your mind didn't always go hand in hand. On the night I'm telling you about, I was glad I'd put on my thickest, most woolly stockings. And I was still shivering, just not as bad as Jack.

"Not my fault if Erik gets himself caught," Jack said. "And I don't want to get caught neither. Hide your hair, Mattie, can't you? It glows brighter than the lamps."

Papa said I had Mama's golden hair and he would never let me cut it. But it wasn't easy to hide it all under a hat. This night I'd borrowed Erik's cap – he had a bigger head than me. I pulled the peak down over my eyes and pushed the shiny strands of hair up inside as best I could.

Jack rubbed at his skinny arms for warmth. In this cold I felt bad that his coat was so worn and thin. Jack looked blue and brittle, and I wished he'd let me lend him my scarf. But he was too proud, like most boys, and wouldn't admit he needed it.

"Where the good goddamn is that boy?" Jack swore.

It made me laugh. Not because he'd cussed, but because Jack called Erik a "boy" when Jack was only twelve himself, just one year older than Erik. I was older than both of them at fourteen.

We poked our heads around the tree trunk again.

Most of Appleton's stores were on College Avenue. The Drug Store, Mr Hooper's Dry Goods Market, Coker and Filliman's Boot-makers – even Doc Lansdale's Dentist's and Barbershop. By day it was the busiest road in town, but at this time of night everything was closed up. Windows were dark, doors were locked.

"Erik's there," I said. "He's coming."

I'd spotted someone coming along the street.

"Hush up," Jack said. "That's not Erik."

And we crouched down real low in the shadows of the tree.

A shabby man with a black, wide-brimmed hat and furry moustache stumbled by. We didn't get many cowboys in these parts. This was Wisconsin, not Texas. But this fellow fit the bill to a "T". And I say he stumbled because he was plainly drunk as a skunk. He must have spent a long evening and a whole heap of dollars in the Brewery House a couple of blocks over. He walked like he had one boot full of lead, the other stuffed with feathers. He was having a drunken confab with an invisible friend.

I thought he wouldn't spot us – that he'd be too far gone to see much past the end of his own nose. But maybe he heard the rattle and chatter of Jack's teeth.

"Who's that there?" the cowboy asked. He spun around so fast I swear I heard the slosh of whiskey in his belly.

Jack gasped and clutched at my arm. And I clutched Jack's right back, just as hard.

"Don't you go sneaking up on me," the cowboy said, sounding real nasty. And then his hand was fumbling under his coat for his holster and pistol.

Me and Jack didn't move an inch. We squatted as low as we could behind that tree. Like I say, we didn't meet many cowboys. Most of the stories we'd heard about them weren't fairy tales. And this cowboy had a gun in his hand.

"I see you," the cowboy said. "I see you there."

We didn't dare breathe in case the cowboy saw the steam in the cold night. Jack was getting set to buck and dash. But I held him back. The cowboy wasn't pointing his gun at us. His googly eyes were peering somewhere over our heads. He was taking aim at the unlit store window behind us.

The cowboy swayed and peered some more, like he didn't quite believe what his eyes were seeing. He was staring in the window of the store behind us – a hat store belonging to the Dannoy sisters. He shuffled a step closer to the window. A step closer to where we were hiding. Then he seemed to cotton on to what it was he was looking at. It was an elegant shop dummy wearing one of the sisters' biggest, frilliest hats. The cowboy blew out a long plume of breath. I reckoned that breath would be strong enough to melt gold bars.

"Damn whiskey making me jumpy," the cowboy muttered. "I knew it was nothing better than cheap gut-rot the second I smelled it."

And with that he stumbled away up Superior Street, grumbling low to his invisible friend.

Me and Jack shivered with relief.

"I'm not waiting longer than one single minute more," Jack whispered to me. "That was too close."

All Jack's belly-aching was getting me worked up real bad too. I was scared what Papa might do if he knew I'd snuck out again. Tan my hide, I'd wager, lady or not.

"If Erik doesn't get here real soon," Jack went on, "I'm going home and you can't stop me."

"He'll get here," I said.

But Jack wasn't so sure. "How do you know he ain't chickened out?"

"Because he's Erik," I said. "He doesn't know how to chicken out."

CHAPTER 2

The Unlocked Doors

At last Erik appeared. Just in time, because me and Jack had almost turned into frozen popsicles under that oak tree.

"He's there, he's there!" I said. "Look!" I pointed across the dark street. "At Hooper's. See?"

"He's not even hiding," Jack said. "He's gonna get us caught." Then, to make sure I knew how annoyed he was, Jack added, "Goddamn it!"

Erik was in front of the locked door to Hooper's Dry Goods Market. He was crouched down with his back to us, but he was plain to see for anyone who might walk by. As we watched, he ran from Mr Hooper's to the butcher's next-but-one along. Then he set to work on that door too.

"He's not even doing it," Jack crowed. "Hooper's door's still closed, look. Erik's all mouth. I knew it. I said to you, didn't I?"

I reckoned Jack didn't want Erik to win his dare. I was thinking Jack had set the dare hoping Erik would fail. I was about to ask him about it, but Erik was scuttling across the street towards us.

Jack sounded angry when he asked Erik, "Where you been for so long?"

Erik looked surprised, as if he thought the answer was an obvious one. "I'm winning our dare," he said. And he ran past us to the door of the Dannoy sisters' hat store. "I just got this one to go."

I followed Erik to the shop's door to watch. At the age of eleven he was short and stocky, more like a tree stump than a barrel. And he could be about as serious as a tree stump too. It wasn't that Erik didn't enjoy jokes, but he sometimes needed them explaining so much that they ended up not being funny any more.

Erik squatted in front of the shop door. He pushed his tangle of black hair out of his eyes and squinted at the door's lock like it was schoolwork set by a mean teacher. He had two bits of wire grasped in his fist. He called them his "picking wires". They were as thin as needles and half a finger long, yet stiff and strong. One was dead straight and hammered flat at the end. One was kinked like a letter "L".

Erik slipped the wires into the keyhole, twisted them, jiggled them. He was focusing so hard that I could tell he was biting his tongue.

He listened to his wires scratch and click inside the lock.

Jack also crept closer to watch him. But Erik hunched over the lock so we couldn't see what he was doing.

It took Erik maybe a minute. Then he jumped up and grinned at us.

"Done," Erik said, and he made a bit of a show of putting his two wires in his shirt pocket.

"Prove it," Jack said with a shrug.

Erik stepped to one side and pointed at the door handle. "Try it," he said.

Jack shrugged again. I was excited, even if Jack was pretending not to give two hoots. So I pushed down on the handle. And the door to the fancy hat store swung wide open, just as if I was a regular customer. Erik grinned wider and

I could see the shine in his bright blue eyes. I laughed out loud.

"Hush up!" Jack said. He grabbed the handle to drag the door shut again. "You want the whole town to think we're breaking in?"

"I'm not breaking in," Erik replied, but his accent had become deeper. It always did when he was angry or worrying about something. Sometimes I forgot that Erik had been born in Hungary, in Europe, but at times like these he sounded most like his papa.

"You dared me to unlock all the shop doors on College Avenue," Erik said to Jack. "You said I couldn't do it, and I have. But I've not set a single foot inside any of them."

Erik was right. That was the dare. I'd told Jack how clever Erik was at opening locks. I'd told him how Erik had got himself into trouble with his mama by unlocking the cookie cupboard for his little brothers and sister – too many times to count. Jack hadn't believed me. And he hadn't believed Erik when he'd shown off his picking wires and boasted about being able to open any door anywhere.

"Oh yeah?" Jack had scoffed. "I bet you couldn't unlock all the doors to the shops on College Avenue."

Jack had just said out loud what had come into his head. I reckoned he'd been joking, but Erik had taken Jack at his word.

"I bet I could," Erik had said without blinking.

Jack had laughed at him. "Hah, never. There's a dozen shops there, I reckon. From Bellamy's Drug Store all the way to the Dannoy sisters' fancy hat place. No way. It's impossible."

"What will I win if I do it?" Erik had asked.

"A white elephant," Jack had joked. "Cos it's impossible. I'm telling you. *Im-poss-ible*. And you wouldn't dare anyway."

"I'll dare all right," Erik had said, and then he'd grinned and asked, "Will you let me join your circus?"

Jack had flinched at that. "It's my circus. I do it by myself."

And he did. Jack might have looked like you could snap him in half, but his dream was to be an acrobat. He could tumble and juggle and walk the low tightrope he strung between two trees at the edge of the park. And those stunts were what Jack called his "circus". He was so serious that each month he spent the last of his money on printed handbills. They read:

Come see Jack Hoefler

King of Tumblers!

Only 5 cents!

Jack gave out the handbills on street corners, but never more than a handful of people came to watch him perform.

"I've been practising how to tumble," Erik had told Jack. "Every day."

Jack had scoffed, but I'd nodded. It was true. I'd seen Erik practising at our shop when Papa wasn't looking.

"I could be an acrobat too," Erik had gone on. "So, when I unlock all the doors to the stores along College Avenue, you have to let me join your circus. That's the deal."

I had known by the look in Jack's eyes that he'd not for one second believed Erik would win the bet. He hadn't even thought Erik would dare to try. But Jack didn't know Erik as well as me.

"OK," Jack had said. "I dare you."

Then the two boys spat on their hands and shook hard, like they were grown-up men of the world.

And that's how we ended up shivering on the corner of College Avenue and Superior Street in the dark.

But Jack still didn't want to admit Erik had won the dare. "We've only seen you unlock this door here," Jack said. "What about all the other doors? You're not tricking me that easy."

"Come on, follow me," Erik said. "You too, Mattie."

Jack and I didn't want to move from our hiding place. But Erik led us into the middle of the street.

"Wait here," he told us. "Watch this."

And then Erik ran to the butcher's door. He checked to make sure we were watching, then he flung the door open. And he went on to Hooper's Dry Goods Market, where he flung that door wide too. Jack and I gasped. And we stared all around, even more scared. What if someone saw now?

Erik didn't care one bat's whisker. He was having too much fun. He ran back across the street and pushed open the door to the Malt Shovel with a single flick of his hand. Then Doc Lansdale's Dentist's and Barbershop. Then Lizzie Cammock's Baker's. Erik ran back and forth from one side of the street to the other, flinging open door after door after door.

"And this one," he shouted and laughed. "This one and this one. I've unlocked every single one!"

But Erik's carefree laughter and the doors banging brought people into the street to see what on earth was going on. Lamps were lit. Sleepy-eyed shopkeepers looked surprised, then shocked, then angry.

“Run!” Jack shouted. And he did just that. He ducked his head and took to his heels.

I stood there, stiffer than a petrified possum. Should I follow Jack or grab Erik and drag him away?

But it came to me in a flash that Erik didn’t want to go anywhere. He didn’t want to escape. Not this time. He wanted people to see this amazing sight. He wanted them to see every shop door along College Avenue flung wide open. He wanted them to gawp and wonder at what he’d done. If Erik ran, he’d never see the looks on their faces. And they’d never know it was him who’d done this amazing thing.

It struck me that in Erik’s mind this was all a performance.

Doc Lansdale stepped into the street, squinty-eyed and raging. His nightshirt was crumpled, and he had his shiny black shotgun in his hands.

"What the hellfire do you think you're doing, boy?" he shouted at Erik.

I made up my own mind right fast on the spot. I followed Jack. I reckoned Erik's performance was more likely to get him a good hiding than a round of applause.

CHAPTER 3

The Sheriff's Handcuffs

If you're anything like me, you might think Erik would have been real glum the next morning. He'd caused such an angry ruckus, such an almighty fuss. Some of the store owners were so furious I reckoned they'd have happily tarred and feathered him. But I guess I shouldn't have been surprised that he was sparky as flint when I saw him. Same as always.

"We got to talk to Jack," Erik told me when I saw him in the back room of our shop. "How about we go and find him when we get a break? I got some ideas for our circus I reckon he'll want to hear."

I spotted how it was now "*our* circus" in Erik's mind, not just Jack's, but didn't say so. Nor did I say that Erik would be lucky if he had a scrap of free time to be in any kind of circus. My papa had punished Erik this morning by giving him all the most horrible chores he could think of. He'd even made Erik swill down the outhouse. Yet Erik hadn't so much as blinked.

I suppose I'd better say that me and Papa ran a store called "Hanover Hardware" on Appleton Avenue. It was a quiet street a few blocks over from College Avenue. We sold lumber and brick, hammers and nails, fence posts and chicken-wire. You needed to build your own house? You came to us. We sold pitch for the walls and tar for the roof. We sold pillows and blankets to make it comfortable, candles and lamps to light it. We even sold locks so you could protect it. Erik spent a lot of time fiddling with the locks. They sure did interest him.

I liked to think me and Papa were a team, but Papa was too bossy and too worried about me behaving all lady-like for that to be true. I had to wear frocks and be pleasant to even the grubbiest customers while Papa fetched and carried what they wanted. That was until he'd cricked his back.

Now Erik did the fetching and carrying. Not me – Papa said no one wanted to see a pretty young girl lugging boxes and sacks. I told Papa I was far from pretty and would soon start running out of young-ness. I reckoned being a strong old woman might be a good thing. But would Papa listen? He said Mama had always been pretty. And that got under my skin worse than a tick, because Mama had died long before she'd had the chance to get very old.

Erik loved his own mama very much. He said she'd carried him all of the way to Appleton from Budapest when he was four. They'd followed after his papa, who was a Rabbi. I wasn't Jewish, so I'd never been to one of Rabbi Weiss's sermons, but I'd heard tell of how he liked to go heavy on the fire and brimstone. Perhaps that's why Rabbi Weiss had struggled to find a proper congregation here. Hellfire talk didn't sit right with a lot of people here in Appleton. This was a young town, a place built upon fresh hope rather than the fear of a vengeful God. And so, back in May, Rabbi Weiss had taken Erik's mama, his four brothers and his tiny sister south to the city of Milwaukee – in search of sinners. But his family were so poor that Erik had stayed behind to work for us at Hanover Hardware. He sent every cent he earned to his mama over a hundred miles away.

Even so, Erik was a boy who dreamed big.

"Thank you for not telling Papa I was with you last night," I said to Erik. We were in the back room of our store. It was damp and chilly and stacked high with a new delivery of bulky crates and cartons. Erik was red-faced and sweaty despite the chill, because Papa had ordered him to stack them all.

"I didn't need to tell him," Erik said. "It wasn't you who unlocked the doors. But I told all the store owners my name. I made sure they'd remember me for our circus. Don't you think if Jack makes some more handbills my name should be on them same as his?"

Erik was still so giddy to be a part of Jack's circus that I hoped Jack would keep his word and let Erik perform. But I hoped even harder that Erik's papa would let him too.

"My papa sent a telegram to yours this morning," I told Erik. I squirmed to be giving bad news. "Papa told him what you did. I asked him not to. But Papa said he felt obliged."

I saw worry flicker in Erik's blue eyes. But it vanished as fast as it appeared.

"My papa knows I want to be an acrobat," Erik said. "He'll be proud that I unlocked all them doors on College Avenue. When I tell him about Jack's circus, he'll understand."

I wondered if "proud" was the right word and just how understanding the "fire and brimstone" Rabbi could be. Not that I was able to say as much because that was when my papa started calling.

"Erik. *Erik!*"

We both ran to the front of the store as I tried to imagine what terrible chore Papa had dreamed up for Erik. I was surprised to see that Papa wasn't alone.

Sheriff Cotter was there too. He had no smile for us. At least I don't think he did behind that thick grey moustache of his. He wore half-moon eye-glasses, and he had a habit of staring over the top of them like you were a bug he'd be happy to squish. But people said the sheriff was fair. And people also said he loved the sound of his own voice as much as he loved locking up criminals.

Sheriff Cotter was leaning on our counter, looking for all the world like it was him who owned our shop. He pushed his glasses higher on his nose as we came out from the back room and fixed his eyes on Erik.

But the sheriff wasn't the biggest surprise. Plonked down on an upturned crate was the drunk cowboy from last night. He looked rougher than if he'd been in a fight with ten angry buffaloes, and lost. His face was pale, his eyes red. The brim of his black hat was creased. His nose was a dark purple bruise, and he had crusty blood at his nostrils and in his moustache. He looked like he'd fallen flat on his face. Splat. He was the best advert not to drink cheap whiskey I'd ever seen. He had his hands clasped together in his lap as if he was praying. But he wasn't. He was wearing handcuffs.

I could tell Papa wasn't happy to have these two men in his store. Our customers were mostly workmen, but Papa kept Hanover Hardware spotless in its looks and its reputation. Papa wore white shirts, bow-ties and round hats from England. He was perhaps the only man in Appleton to scrape his face clean of whiskers twice a day.

Papa said, "Sheriff Cotter wants to talk to you, Erik."

I felt my heart give a kick like a mule. But when I looked at Erik, he just smiled at the sheriff.

"How can I help, sir?" Erik asked. His voice was so calm that his accent didn't even show.

"So you're the young'un who made all that fuss on College Avenue last night, is that right?" Sheriff Cotter asked.

Erik nodded, and his smile slipped a bit. "I didn't mean any harm. And I didn't damage any of the doors or the locks. I was only –"

The sheriff waved his hand to hush Erik. "I'm not here about that – other than to warn you not to do it again. And I'll be blowed trying to work out how it got into your head to pull such a stunt. You might not have made many friends from them store owners, but I reckon you done one or two a favour in the long run. Got them thinking. If a boy like you can open their doors, then a scoundrel like this one here could break in without breaking a sweat." He pointed at the cowboy as he said it. "I wouldn't be surprised if you sold a few of your finest locks over the next couple of days, Mr Hanover. So, I'm not fussed about last night, son, but I am here on related business."

Me and Papa were more than a little glad to hear the sheriff wasn't going to arrest Erik for last night. But Erik didn't look glad at all.

"Oh no, sir," Erik said with a frown. "This man could never open all those locks. I'm the only one who could do it. That's why –"

"*Erik!*" Papa hissed. "Hush, boy."

"But I'm just telling Sheriff Cotter the truth, Mr Hanover." Erik was set on taking full credit, even if it meant another swill of the outhouse. "I'm the only one who could have opened all those doors and –"

The sheriff cut Erik off by saying, "There was a robbery last night, but it wasn't anything to do with your antics. And they used a gun – didn't pick any locks."

I was shocked. "A robbery? Here?" I said. Papa scowled at me for speaking out, but I needed to know more. I'd never heard of such a thing in Appleton. "What was stolen?" I asked.

"Nothing from any store on College Avenue," the sheriff repeated. "But all the wages from the paper mill are gone. Some low-belly snake just upped and disappeared with the safe full of money. There's fathers who won't be able to feed their children at the end of the week now."

Sheriff Cotter prodded the drunken cowboy with the toe of his boot. "All the people who saw it said the thief looked just like this good-for-nothing right here. Mr Gus Boydell from Chicago. And I knew who they meant. I've had my eye on him. So I wasn't slow to arrest him. But now there's been far too many witnesses said they saw him, nowhere near the paper mill, but drunk in the Brewery House and around the 2nd Ward."

"He was on College Avenue last night," I said. I'd opened my mouth without thinking.

Papa's scowl deepened. "And how do you know that, young lady?"

"Erik told me," I mumbled as I went redder than a hot beet.

Erik looked confused, but I glared at him and he kept his mouth shut.

Papa tutted but didn't ask me more.

The sheriff blew out a big breath. "There you go. Another witness tells me you were elsewhere," he said to the cowboy. "I've heard of lucky drunks before, but you float the whole barrel, Mr Boydell."

Sheriff Cotter turned back to Erik. "I don't pardon what you did last night, sonny. But more than that, I don't enjoy men like Mr Gus Boydell stinking up my town. I'll be more than happy to see him gone. Only, when I went to get him out of the cuffs this morning, blow me if I hadn't gone and lost my key. So, after that mischief you were up to last night, I'm hoping I've come to the right person. See what I'm driving at, young Erik?" the sheriff said. "I'm asking if you think you're clever enough to get these cuffs open."

"I never opened handcuffs before," Erik said. But I could see by the look on his face that he was itching to try. "I never even *seen* handcuffs before, to tell the truth."

"I can cut them off," Papa told the sheriff. "Mattie, why don't you fetch me a saw?"

"No, no," Sheriff Cotter said. "I'd like to keep my cuffs in one piece if I can, in case I find that key. Let's see the boy try." Then the sheriff leaned in close to the battered cowboy and said, "You try anything funny while the young'un's at it and I'll make you real sorry. Understand?"

Gus Boydell gritted his yellow teeth and turned away.

The sheriff smacked him round the head like it was a bell. The cowboy's hungover eyes clanged in their sockets.

"I asked you if you *understand*?" the sheriff snarled.

Boydell nodded fast.

We could all see it hurt his head to do it.

So Sheriff Cotter stepped aside to let Erik get close. He took his picking wires out of his shirt pocket and crouched down to inspect the handcuffs on Boydell's wrists. We all leaned as close as we could to watch Erik as he set to work on the small lock. Even the cowboy stared.

But Erik shook his head. "My wires are too big for this lock," he said. "Could you get me some thinner wire, Mr Hanover?"

Papa wasn't happy to be the one asked to fetch and carry. But I could tell he didn't want to refuse Erik in front of the sheriff. Papa snipped an inch or two of chicken wire, and Erik bent it into a hooked "L" shape. Then he set to work again.

We could hear the scratch and click of the thin wire inside the lock. Erik was biting on his bottom lip. He didn't look at the lock as he worked, but cocked his head and listened. Papa started to say something, but Erik told him to "Hush up, please." Erik was never less than polite, but his words still sent Papa red in the face. I wondered if Erik might pay for it later.

We'd leaned even closer, the three of us now peering over Erik. He was taking much longer with these handcuffs than he had with the lock I'd seen him open on College Avenue. So long in fact that Papa again offered to fetch a saw for the sheriff.

Sheriff Cotter shook his head. Then he shrugged. He was looking like someone who thought he was going to need a new pair of handcuffs after all.

At last Erik rocked back on his heels and stood up. He stretched his back and rolled his neck, relaxing his tensed muscles. He stepped away from the cowboy and blew out his breath. He put his picking wires back in his pocket.

But Gus Boydell was still locked into the handcuffs. We all sort of sagged, feeling disappointed.

"Ah, well," Sheriff Cotter said to Erik. "Thank you for trying."

"They're unlocked," Erik told him. "They're a bit stiff is all."

We watched as the cowboy flexed his wrists. The handcuffs fell off his lap and rattled to the floor.

The sheriff's grin couldn't have been wider. "Well, how about that?" Sheriff Cotter said. "If that don't beat everything." He clapped Erik on the back so hard that Erik staggered. "This boy deserves a bonus in his pay packet this week, Hanover," the sheriff told Papa.

And even Papa laughed at that. (But he never did add that extra bonus to Erik's pay.)

We were all grinning and patting Erik on the back. We'd never seen such a thing. We told Erik how amazing he was. Except for the cowboy. His narrow eyes were bloodshot and dazed, but he was staring at Erik like he was a juicy steak. A big juicy steak sitting on a golden plate. I'd never seen such a look in a man's eyes. It chilled me worse than the icy weather outside. But I told myself not to worry. Not with Sheriff Cotter right there with us.

"How'd you do it?" the sheriff asked Erik. He picked up his handcuffs, then shook his head as he examined them.

Erik shrugged. "I like locks," he said. "I like to know how they work. Please, if you have an old pair of handcuffs, or if you don't find the key to this pair, can I have them so I can practise some more?"

"That's a deal," Sheriff Cotter said. He laughed again. "I wish my constables had been here to see such a thing. I don't reckon they're going to believe it. I don't reckon I would if I hadn't been right here and seen it with my own eyes."

The sheriff's grey moustache twitched as he smiled at Erik. But then he scowled when he turned to Gus Boydell, who was still slumped on the crate.

I'm not too proud to say that that cowboy scared me. He looked beat-up, but I could see he was taking real sharp interest in Erik. He never took his red-rimmed eyes off my friend. It was clear to me he wasn't thinking pleasant thoughts, even if Erik had freed him from the cuffs.

"Right this minute," the sheriff went on, "I got to throw this trash out of town." He dragged Boydell off the crate and across the floor. "And, Erik, if I get you some handcuffs, you'll promise to leave Appleton's store owners to sleep peaceful at night, won't you?"

"Yes, sir," Erik said.

The sheriff nodded, then shoved Boydell out of our shop and into the street.

I saw Gus Boydell stare back at Erik as he tumbled out the door and onto the sidewalk.

CHAPTER 4

The Two Tickets

Jack's skinny face peered in at our store's front window. He waved at me.

I hoped Papa didn't see him. He said Jack was a lout. But I didn't think that was fair. It wasn't Jack's fault he was a shoeshine boy who never seemed to have more than two buttons to his name. Sometimes he was so hard-up he had to collect his old Five-Cent Circus handbills that people had tossed away. He couldn't afford new ones, so spent hours searching the litter in the alleys for any scrunched-up sheets of paper with his name on them. Then he ironed them flat and snipped off any ripped corners to make them neat again.

Jack had told me, “I've shined shoes that cost more to buy than I earn in a whole month. But maybe when I'm a famous showman with a proper circus I'll wear rich-man's shoes too.”

Papa didn't want me being friends with shoeshine boys or circus performers. For someone who sold shovels for a living, Papa could be such a snob. But he didn't spot Jack peering in the window because Papa was too busy charming the Dannoy sisters.

I don't reckon the sisters had ever set one of their fussy feet in our store before. Constance Dannoy was wearing a hat with so many feathers I expected it to lay eggs. She was holding a heavy padlock in one hand and a big deadbolt in the other.

“You believe you could open both of these?” Constance asked Erik in her creaky old voice.

Erik nodded. “Oh yes. Definitely.”

Constance made a noise of dismay at the back of her throat. She turned to her younger sister, Patience. Her hat had so many bows and ribbons it looked like a birthday present for the Queen of England.

“How will we ever feel safe again?” Constance whimpered.

Sheriff Cotter had been right about one thing – all of a sudden everybody wanted to buy the best locks they could from our shop. But what the sheriff hadn’t counted on was Erik’s honesty. I had watched it flummox several customers.

Earlier that day Doc Lansdale had left empty-handed. He’d declared, “I ain’t buying a lock some eleven-year-old tyke can outwit.”

Now, Papa stepped in between Erik and the sisters. “Never you worry, ladies,” Papa said. “These are indeed the finest quality locks.” He jabbed Erik with an elbow and shooed him to one side. “Haven’t you got some boxes to stack?” Papa asked.

“I’ve got a job for Erik,” I said to Papa.

When Papa was talking to the sisters again, I waved at Jack, pointing so he knew to meet us around the back of our store.

“I was only telling the truth,” Erik said as I pulled him along with me. “I’m pretty sure I could open all the locks your papa sells.”

“I believe you,” I said. “But no one else understands that you’re the only person in the whole of Wisconsin – if not the whole of America – who could.”

“The whole of America?” Erik asked. “You really think so?”

"Who else forgets to sleep at night because they're so busy playing with locks?" I said.

"I'm not playing. I'm learning," Erik told me.

"I guess that's my point."

In the back room I opened the door to the yard, letting in October's chilly wind. Jack was shivering and fast to dodge inside. I closed the door and gave him a horse blanket to wrap around his body for warmth.

Jack grinned his thanks. "I got some real great news," he said. "Bet you can't guess." He was so excited he didn't wait for me to try. "What are you doing tomorrow night, Mattie?" Jack asked. "Want to go to the theatre?"

You could have knocked me down with Constance Dannoy's feather hat. "The theatre?" I asked.

"That's right," Jack said. "Me and you. Like posh folks."

"Really? How?"

Jack was frothing like fresh beer, so eager he was to tell the story. "I had this English fellow in my shoeshine chair. He sounded like a lord or something, the way he spoke. He talked to me and I told him that I wasn't just a shoeshine boy but a circus performer too. And guess what?" Jack was almost drunk with glee, and I had to hush him so my papa wouldn't hear.

"Sorry," Jack whispered. "Sorry." Then, in another gush of words he added, "He only went and said that he's a performer too. Said he's a master magician, from England, and he's travelling all around and doing a big show at the theatre here in town tomorrow night. He reckoned I polished his shoes the best he's ever seen and gave me two tickets to his show. So we gotta go, right? Me and you?"

And Jack waved the two tickets at me like it was him doing a magic trick.

To be honest, I was too stunned to answer. I stared at the tickets with my mouth wide open.

"So I can be in your circus, then?" Erik asked. It was almost as if he hadn't heard anything Jack had just said. "Like you said I could?"

Now it was Jack's turn to be stunned into silence. Or maybe it was more "embarrassed".

"Sorry I ran out on you last night," Jack said to Erik at last. "I thought you was going to get caught."

"Erik did get caught," I said. "I ran away too."

"I didn't get caught," Erik said, confused. "I let everyone know it was me."

“Same difference,” I said. Then to Jack, “But the fuss is pretty much over now. Papa’s forgiven Erik because now he’s selling extra locks nobody needs.”

Jack laughed with delight at the town’s store owners wasting their money.

“But you haven’t heard the best bit yet ...” I said.

And I told Jack all about Gus Boydell, the robbery at the paper mill, and the lost key to Sheriff Cotter’s handcuffs.

“A robbery?” Jack said. “Here in Appleton?” And he looked at Erik. “That’s some skill you’ve got there to open those handcuffs, I’ll admit to that.”

“So can I be in your circus?” Erik said, as persistent as ever. “I did your dare and won our bet. I’ve been doing my acrobat training. Want to see me bend over backwards and pick a pin up with my teeth?"

Jack looked at his feet – at his shoes that had never seen even a lick of polish.

"Problem is," Jack said, "I'm an acrobat. My circus don't need two, you see. And I can do the pin trick myself."

"That's what I was thinking," Erik said. "So, instead of your tightrope between the trees, how about we set up a trapeze?"

Jack didn't much like that idea. "I always walk the tightrope," he said. "It's my best trick."

"But my trick would be better," Erik told him. "I reckon I could pick up a pin with my teeth while swinging on a trapeze."

"You've never swung on a trapeze," Jack said.

"I could learn."

“We don’t even have a trapeze,” Jack said. It was clear he was trying to have the last word. “It’s a stupid idea.”

But I was watching Jack. I don’t think he thought it was a stupid idea at all. I think he was fretting that Erik might be able to do what he said he could and then Jack wouldn’t have the best trick in his own circus any more.

Erik hung his head at the word “stupid”. He hadn’t been kidding – his heart had been set on being part of Jack’s circus.

“Look, if you’re so desperate, how about you unlock something?” Jack suggested.

“Unlock what?” Erik asked.

“I don’t know,” Jack said. “A padlock. Or maybe some handcuffs? But do it for everyone at the circus to see.”

"I saw him with the sheriff's handcuffs," I said. "And it's not very exciting."

Jack and Erik sighed. They both knew I was right.

"I'm sorry, kid," Jack said. "Two acrobats is one too many, right?"

"But you said I could be in your circus," Erik pleaded. I could hear the accent strong now in his voice. "I just had to unlock the shop doors on College Avenue."

"I know, I know," Jack said. "But I didn't think you'd really do it."

"Erik didn't just do it," I said. "He never told anyone that it was you who dared him to."

Jack squirmed, and his face went hot with shame. I could see he was chewing over something tough in his mind as we stood in silence. Until at last Jack pushed the two theatre tickets he was holding into my hand.

"Here," Jack said. "You have them both. You two go."

"But ..." I said. "They were given to you. Don't you want to go?"

"The magician showed me a trick with some cards anyway," Jack told me. "While I shined his shoes. And it wasn't that great. I reckon I could goddamn guess how it was done anyways."

And with that Jack shrugged off the horse blanket and ducked out the door into the cold of the back yard.

"Well, that's maybe the kindest thing I've ever known Jack Hoefler do," I said to Erik as I held the two tickets tight. I was hoping I could talk Papa into letting us go.

But Erik's thoughts were sometimes like stubborn mules stuck in the mud. He asked, "Do you think I could be an acrobat who unlocks locks at the same time as swinging on a trapeze?"

CHAPTER 5

The English Magician

The show was incredible.

Astounding.

Amazing!

We saw a thousand beautiful butterflies appear in thin air. We saw chairs float and dance above the stage. We saw a woman cut into pieces and put back together again. All right before our very eyes!

The magician's name was Dr Lynn, and he glided across the stage like the most dapper man I'd ever seen. His English accent sounded like silk compared to the rough way we talked in these parts. His suit was as black as midnight and his shirt as white as an angel's cloud. And he made everyone packed into the Appleton Grand Theatre believe he had miraculous powers – powers that would make the Devil himself grind his teeth with envy.

At first, me and Erik had felt out of place in the plush theatre. But we had tickets just like everyone else, so we sat back and enjoyed the show. When it ended, we didn't want to leave. While everybody left, we felt stuck to our seats. We talked about how Dr Lynn had performed his miracles. But we couldn't guess his secrets. So Erik said, "I'm going to ask him."

We headed outside and around to the stage door on a side street. There were two burly men loading worn crates into a dark, covered carriage. We both reckoned that Dr Lynn's secrets were inside those crates. On the doors of the carriage were the words "Dr Lynn" in flashy curls and loops. The horses at the reins were blowing steam in the cold, wanting to be away.

"Enjoy the show?" a voice said, making us both jump.

I turned around and saw the voice belonged to Jack.

"It was amazing," I told him. "Thank you for the tickets. Thank you thank you thank you, Jack." I actually hugged him. "It was the best thing ever."

"I wish you'd seen it too, Jack," Erik said. "I bet you everything you would have been just as amazed as us."

"I did see it," Jack said with a grin. "I may not be able to open locks. But who needs to if a back window's been left open?"

"You sneaked in?" asked Erik.

I couldn't tell if Erik was impressed or horrified.

"Of course I did," Jack said. "I wasn't gonna miss it for anything. Did you see the way he chopped up that woman with those swords? But then she got put back together again? I'd like to do something like that in my circus. I bet I could charge more than five cents if I did that!"

And I jumped a second time when a hand touched my arm.

"Careful, my dear," a silky English voice said. "You'll be the poor soul he's dreaming of cutting into bits."

And this time the voice was Dr Lynn – behind us, as if he'd appeared from out of nowhere. Like magic. He was wearing a heavy black cloak and carried a dark walking stick with a silver top that glittered in the light of the gas lamps.

"Hello, my shoeshine friend," Dr Lynn said to Jack.

Jack mumbled "Hello", with a shifty look on his face. I guessed he was wondering if Dr Lynn had overheard how he'd snuck in.

But if the magician had heard, he didn't mention it. To be honest, Dr Lynn didn't have time to because Erik was already hurling questions at him.

"How did you make the chairs float?" Erik asked. "I thought it might be wires, but how were they attached? Are the butterflies real or made of paper? When you cut up that woman, can she feel it? And –"

The magician held up his hands as if begging for mercy. "Please, please. I'm drowning in questions."

"But I need to know," Erik told Dr Lynn. In his excitement his accent was stronger than ever. "I want to be a magician too. As good as you."

"I'll take that as a compliment," Dr Lynn said. "But my secrets are my secrets."

Erik looked ready to explode, like a stubby stick of dynamite. "I won't tell anyone," Erik promised. "I won't! But –"

The magician struck his walking stick against the cobbles at his feet. The metal tip sparked in the dark. The horses whinnied, and we all jumped back. Erik was finally hushed.

"I applaud your enthusiasm," Dr Lynn told him. "But secrets have to be earned, not taken. How do I know you'll put this fair lady back together again if I give you the secret of how to cut her into pieces?" Dr Lynn clapped his hands as if he'd been struck by a sudden, powerful thought. "Can you read?" he asked. "Of course you can. So I recommend a book to you. *The Memoirs of Jean Eugene Robert-Houdin*. Find it. Read it. He was the greatest conjurer the world has ever seen. Let him teach you, if you're able to learn. But now I must go. Another town and another audience awaits." Dr Lynn's midnight cloak twirled as he turned to his carriage.

"Thank you, Dr Lynn," Jack called. "Thank you for the tickets, sir."

The magician stopped before he climbed into the carriage, and looked back at the three of us. "Didn't I give you *two* tickets?" he asked, with a wry smile.

We scuttled away, talking as we walked fast back to Appleton Avenue and Papa's store. The night seemed to grow chillier by the second.

I had to promise Erik that we'd go to the library as soon as my papa would let us and look for the book Dr Lynn had told us to read. But still Erik was disappointed that he hadn't learned any real secrets.

Jack said goodnight at the corner of Appleton Avenue, and I thanked him for the tickets again. I sensed he wanted another hug. So I gave him one. It made him smile so wide he looked like a drunk frog. I don't mind admitting his skinny but strong arms made me smile too.

I was still smiling when Erik asked, "Who's that waiting for us?"

My smile vanished in a snap, faster than any magic trick.

We could see the shape of a man in front of the window of Hanover Hardware. The lights were still lit inside, so we couldn't see the man's face. Just the shape of a shabby cowboy hat.

We knew exactly who it was.

Gus Boydell crossed the street towards us.

Why was he waiting for us? What could he want?

But before Gus Boydell got to us, the door to our shop opened and another man stepped out. Boydell flinched, cursed, then ducked back into the shadows before he was seen by the other man.

We could see the other man in the bright doorway. He was tall and broad with an old face and a thick grey beard. He spoke, but in a language I didn't understand.

Erik replied to the man, "Yes, Papa. Coming, Papa."

CHAPTER 6

The Overheard Conversation

I knew I wasn't going to get any sleep that night. I sat wrapped in blankets at my window, watching the shadows in Appleton Avenue below.

Was that Boydell? Or was that him moving over there? I'd tried to tell Papa how we'd seen the cowboy, but he'd dismissed it as all my imagination, saying it must have been another cowboy who just looked like Boydell.

"The sheriff saw that rascal off," Papa said. "He wouldn't dare come back here."

The night got later, and I wanted to fetch a glass of water from the kitchen. But the kitchen was also where Erik slept, and tonight he was still awake talking with his papa. I didn't want to disturb them just for a glass of water.

I sat at the top of the stairs. The candle light flickered round the edges of the kitchen door, and the voices escaped that way too. Maybe if I was a proper lady like my papa wanted me to be I wouldn't have listened in to what they were saying.

Rabbi Weiss spoke in a mixture of Hungarian – his home-tongue – and English. I knew that Erik could understand Hungarian but he hadn't spoken it since he'd been little. It was because Erik didn't like anyone to know he was an immigrant. He'd been bullied by other boys in Appleton and made to feel ashamed. But I'd said almost everyone we knew in America had been some kind of immigrant at one time or another.

I had told Erik my great-grandaddy had come here from Europe too – and look how German Jack's name is, I'd said. But Erik wanted people to think he'd been born here in brand new Appleton rather than ancient Budapest on the shores of the Danube. I'd told Erik it was the bullies who should feel both stupid *and* shameful, not him.

"You have caused many people a lot of upset," I heard Rabbi Weiss say to Erik in the kitchen.

"Sheriff Cotter said I've done the storekeepers a good deed," Erik replied. "And Mr Hanover is very happy with all of his new lock sales."

"All the same," Rabbi Weiss said, "you will come back to Milwaukee with me in the morning."

“I can’t,” Erik said. “Not until I’ve performed in Jack’s circus.”

“Erik, you are not a circus boy,” his papa told him. “You are the son of a Rabbi.”

“But I *want* to perform. I’ve been training so hard as an acrobat, Papa. Every day. But now I want to be like Dr Lynn, the magician we saw at the theatre tonight. You would have called what he did *miracles*.”

“Maybe they were miracles,” Rabbi Weiss said. “Maybe he is a man of God.”

“No, they’re tricks,” Erik said. “Or not just tricks. Illusions. Cleverer than miracles.”

“Erik! Don’t say such a thing!”

“But the tricks, they are like locks. And knowing how they work is a key to their mystery.”

"Why must you take everything apart?" Rabbi Weiss said to his son. "Isn't there more joy to leave them as mysteries?"

"No. I must know how they work. Because then I can perform them too."

I knew Erik and his father would always love each other dearly, but it was clear they would never truly understand one another.

And of course that made me think about how my own papa talked – and talked – about how I must be a lady. But Papa's idea of a lady was so very narrow when compared to mine. And I wondered if every parent dreamed different dreams to their children.

Rabbi Weiss sounded like he was losing patience with his son.

"*Again* I say you are not a performer," I heard him say. "*Again* I have to tell you that you are the son of a Rabbi. *This* is the life God has given you."

"I want more," Erik said. "Why can't I have more? It is wrong of God to make us poor, to make Mama fret over food and to make you ill with worry. Mr Hanover is kind, but he'll never make me so rich as to truly help you and Mama. If I was a performer, we could have carriages and clothes as expensive as Dr Lynn's. I promise, one day I'll bring golden coins to Mama and she'll never have to worry again."

"But this is not God's plan for us," his papa said.

"Then God will have to make another plan," Erik insisted. "Or I'll make one for myself without Him."

Rabbi Weiss's sudden rush of angry words shocked me away from the door. I heard a chair fall over and the Rabbi jumping to his feet. I couldn't see, but I imagined him waving his fist and making threats of hellfire.

"But I can't leave," Erik said, and I could hear tears in his voice. "I can't. Please don't make me, Papa."

Yet more angry Hungarian words made me run back to my room. I felt like a terrible intruder. This was between a father and his son. I decided I'd manage very well without a glass of water tonight.

But I still couldn't sleep. I knew how Erik would feel if he didn't get to perform in the Five-Cent Circus.

CHAPTER 7

The Twins

It felt even frostier inside than outside the next morning.

Erik and his papa hardly spoke to each other at breakfast. Then Rabbi Weiss returned to Milwaukee alone. But not before Erik made him a promise.

"I've promised to go to Milwaukee too," Erik told me later. "Papa thinks it will be better for me to be closer to him. And I suppose I have missed being with Mama and my sister and brothers. So it's a good thing, isn't it?"

But Erik's face didn't look like he thought it was a good thing, and I had no answer for his question.

"When do you have to go?" I said instead. I didn't want him to leave. Next to Jack, Erik was my best friend.

"I told Papa I must help your father while he's so busy. And so I can stay here until the end of the week. I'll leave on Monday's train."

And saying that, Erik smiled.

I reckoned I could guess why. "So you can be in Jack's circus on Sunday?" I asked.

Erik nodded. "If Jack will let me."

"Don't worry," I said. "We'll make sure he does."

For the rest of that morning, trade at Hanover Hardware was slow, and so Papa went out to fit all those new locks he'd sold. I told Erik I was happy to look after the store if he wanted to go to the library to look for the book Dr Lynn had told us about. And he dashed off, eager to do just that.

When Erik returned, he didn't just have the book but Jack was with him too. They vanished into the back room with the book while I sold two sacks of coal to Henry Bowerton and a new pan to Old Lady Linthorn. All the time I felt jealous that the boys were unlocking the mysteries of the universe.

At last I went to join them. They were on their knees with the book open on the floor in front of them. It looked like a rather normal book to me, but they didn't even glance up when I walked in. Jack turned a page. They read together. Then Erik turned a page.

"What secrets have you discovered?" I asked.

"He led an amazing life," Erik said.

"He was from France," Jack said, "and he performed conjuring tricks for kings and queens."

"But he was just normal and worked as a clerk when he was young," Erik explained.

"But he became a magician and was then the most famous man in all of Europe," Jack added.

"He led an amazing life."

"You've already told me that, Erik," I said. "And what was this miraculous man's name again?"

"Jean Eugene Robert-Houdin," Erik said, his accent mangling the French name.

"And does Monsieur Robert-Houdin tell you how to chop someone into little pieces without killing them?" I asked.

They both shook their heads. They didn't seem to care about that. This conjuror's life story had Jack and Erik gaping in wonder as they read.

"We need conjuring tricks in my circus," Jack said.

"I could do some," Erik told him.

"I thought you wanted to be an acrobat with a trapeze."

"I thought there was only room for one acrobat – and that was you."

I heard the *ding* of the bell above the shop door – there was a new customer for me to serve. I left the boys to their story of Robert-Houdin. But there was no customer waiting for me out front. It was a shabby cowboy I'd hoped I'd never see again.

Gus Boydell grabbed me hard, snatching at my wrist as I tried to run. I screamed.

Erik and Jack burst in from the back room the second they heard me.

"Fetch the sheriff!" I yelled. "Fetch the sheriff!"

"Not you, clever boy," Boydell said to Erik. He drew his pistol and pointed it at him. Its deadly barrel pinned Erik to the spot. "You're the one I'm after," Boydell growled.

But Jack was gone. I prayed he'd run like the wind to find Sheriff Cotter.

"I've got a cart outside," Boydell said. He licked his dry lips as if he was nervous. His dirty moustache glistened with spit. "Now, you two are not going to give me any trouble –

none at all, you hear? Unless you want to catch yourselves some hot lead." He waved his pistol to be sure we understood his meaning. "You're going to come with me to that cart – real quiet, real easy – and get down under the blankets on the back of it. OK? I don't want no one seeing you. *OK?*"

My breath was trapped deep in my chest with fear. I was gasping like a fish in a net. I dared to look at Erik and saw he was whiter than ghostly milk.

We let ourselves be taken outside by Boydell. There was no one in the street, and we climbed onto the back of his cart and under the blankets like he'd told us. We could hear Jack shouting for help on the next street over, yelling for Sheriff Cotter.

"I should have put a bullet in that loudmouth to shut him up," Boydell hissed, and flicked the reins on his horse. The cart clattered along at a jolting, uncomfortable speed.

Under the filthy blankets, we had no idea where he was taking us. We grasped each other's hands, too scared to move as we banged about on the cart bed. I didn't think Boydell would have been able to hear us over the clatter of his horse and cart, but we never spoke a word. We held hands tight and stared into each other's eyes.

It wasn't long before we could hear the rushing sound of the Fox River. It was wide and strong enough to power the paper mill that had been built on its far bank. Next we heard the rumble of a wooden bridge under the cart's wheels, and we both knew Boydell was taking us out of town.

We left the bridge and the river behind, and the cart bumped along a rutted track, its wheels quieter now across the muddy ground. I had lost any hope that the sheriff was close behind us. Boydell had snatched us much too fast. He'd kidnapped us and no one knew where we were! With that thought, plus the stink of the blankets and the rattle of the cart, I thought I might vomit with terror.

Erik was trying to look out from under the blanket. I shook my head at him – I was scared Boydell would see him. But Erik lifted the edge of the blanket and peered out to see the way we'd come. Maybe I should have been comforted that he was thinking of escape, but my whirling, tumbling mind wouldn't let me.

At last the cart came to a stop, and Erik let the blanket fall back down. We heard Boydell grunt as he climbed off the driver's seat and his boots thudded on the ground.

"I got the one we wanted," he said, as if he was talking to someone who'd been waiting for him. "But I had to bring another along too or she would have yelled the whole place down."

"Won't make no difference," a second voice said, which sounded very much like Boydell's. "They can both end up the same way."

The blanket was whipped off us.

I saw that we were in a clearing in the woods. There was an old shack with busted windows and no door to speak of – just a blanket hanging in the frame. In front of the shack was a black metal box. Boydell was sitting on it, his legs wide apart and grinning like he was riding his favourite horse. No, I realised, this wasn't a box. A safe. Boydell really had stolen the wages from the paper mill.

But how could he have done it when Jack and I had seen him so drunk on College Avenue that same night?

I looked again at Boydell sitting on the safe, and I looked at him hard.

All of a sudden I understood how he'd fooled the sheriff. It was as if he'd performed his own magic trick. This man wasn't Gus Boydell at all. Gus Boydell was leaning on the cart behind us. This other man was his twin brother.

CHAPTER 8

The Kiss

"So you're the wonder boy my brother's been telling me about, are you?" Boydell the Second said. "You can open locks? Pick them, is that right? All and any locks?"

Erik didn't answer him. We were still on the back of the cart. It was colder than cold. But I reckon it was fear as well as cold that was making me shudder so bad.

"Come here," Boydell the Second told Erik.

But Erik didn't move.

Gus Boydell poked Erik in the back with his pistol. "I'd do what my brother Jimmy says if you know what's good for you. His nature ain't quite as honey-sweet as mine."

Slowly, like his legs were soft instead of bony, Erik climbed down off the cart. He walked up to Jimmy Boydell sitting on the safe.

"Reckon you can open this safe?" Jimmy asked.

Erik shrugged, then shook his head.

The safe was in a battered state. It looked like the brothers had been at it with hammers and chisels and who knew what else.

"Maybe if you open it, maybe we let you go," Jimmy said. "Up to you."

"It's a different type of lock," Erik said. But he stumbled over his words, his fear strengthening his Hungarian accent and tying up his tongue.

Jimmy leaned in real close to Erik. "What's that? What's that you're saying?" And Jimmy snarled at his brother, "Jeez, Gus. You never told me he was a foreign kid."

"Didn't know meself," Gus said.

"Ah well." Jimmy grinned a filthy, broken grin. "No one's gonna care if we kill a grubby foreign kid, are they? Makes life a bit easier if you ask me. People will thank us for doing a bit of cleaning up."

"A safe has a different type of lock," Erik repeated in a pleading voice. "I don't know how to open them."

"Try," Jimmy Boydell said.

"I don't –" Erik started to say.

"Try or you might not be going home tonight."

Erik's hands trembled as he went to take his picking wires out of his shirt pocket. But the wires weren't there.

"I don't have my wires," Erik said after he'd checked his pants pockets too. I could see he was trying hard not to sob. "They're gone."

"Your what?" Jimmy Boydell asked. "You trying to pull a fast one, kid?"

But Gus said, "Yeah, the kid uses these tiny wires to pick locks. I guess he can't do it without them."

"I've lost them," Erik said. "They've fallen out of my pocket. I don't know where they are."

Jimmy searched Erik's pockets, all rough and angry. He looked as distrustful as a twice-kicked cat.

"So you brought me this goddamn useless foreign kid," Jimmy said to his brother. "Two days I've been waiting here with this safe." He slapped the safe with the palm of his hand and cursed. "I reckon you were still drunk when you thought this was such a goddamn good idea –"

"You got a better idea?" Gus said.

"Yeah," Jimmy replied. "Let's get rid of these two kids and get us some explosives. Then we'll get this thing open."

"And how should I get rid of them?" Gus asked.

"What do I care?" Jimmy said. "But don't waste my bullets. We might need all we've got if this pig's-ear mess gets any worse."

“So what should I do?” Gus asked.

Jimmy Boydell turned away and ducked past the blanket into the old shack. He came back with chains and padlocks in a rusty tangle. “I don’t want them blabbing to anybody about us being out here in the woods. Wrap ’em up with these to weigh ’em down and chuck ’em in the river. That way, no one will ever find their bodies.”

Gus took the chains off his brother. “Ain’t we gonna need these to carry the safe on the cart again?”

Jimmy rolled his eyes and said, “Why would we want to carry the safe after we’ve blown it open?”

Gus shrugged and nodded. But then he thought of something else. “And how’s this gonna work if the kid can pick locks?” he asked.

Jimmy looked like he was about ready to chuck his brother in the river too. "How's he gonna pick the locks if he's not got his wires or whatever they are? Let's just get it done fast."

Next thing we knew, the brothers had wrapped us in the chains so tight that it hurt. I felt like my very bones were being crushed. But that wasn't why I cried. I sobbed and begged them to let us go. But they didn't listen. They didn't care.

They tossed us like a sack of kittens onto the cart and drove us out of the woods back down towards the river. Both me and Erik struggled and kicked and thrashed and fought, but there was no way we could get those chains off. They weren't just tight but heavy. Our hands were pinned down at our waists with padlocks as big as a butcher's fist.

All I could think was that I'd never been so frightened before. I was dizzy with fear as we were bounced on that cart towards the river bank. I felt so weak I could do nothing but lie down on the cart-bed and pray with all my heart. I prayed that Papa or the sheriff or even Jack would appear to save us. My whole face was wet with snot and tears.

Next to me, Erik was squirming on his belly. I thought he was trying to shake off the chains – to wriggle out of them. But then he was gripping the filthy blanket with his teeth. He shook it like an angry dog. I didn't know what he was doing, but I could see that he was very focused, very determined. He was brave, but I didn't know what good his bravery would do him. I carried on with my prayers.

We reached the bank of the Fox River, and I could see our town of Appleton over the other side. I decided that if Erik could be brave, so could I. I started to holler for help. I was ready to shout myself hoarse if it meant someone across the wide river would hear. But Jimmy Boydell smacked me hard around the head to silence me.

I fell face down onto the cart. And then I saw it ... Right there ... Right in front of me ...

In a flash I knew what Erik had been doing when he'd pulled at the blanket with his teeth. He'd been looking for the picking wires that had fallen out of his shirt pocket and onto the bed of the cart. And there was one of them right in front of my eyes.

I licked and bit at that little "L" of wire, not caring how many splinters I got in my tongue. At last I had it between my teeth.

At that moment, the Boydell brothers jumped down from the cart's front seat. Before they could grab us, I lunged at Erik and kissed him full on the lips.

"Aw, ain't that sweet," one of the brothers laughed. I think it was Gus.

Whoever it was, he then shoved me hard in the side, and I tumbled and slid off the cart like a sack of coal. I screamed as I hit the icy, rushing water of the Fox River. I wished I'd had time to hold my breath.

But at least in that kiss I'd given Erik the chance to save us.

CHAPTER 9

The First Escape

The water was like a pickaxe of ice being driven into my heart. The heavy chains dragged me down among freezing bursts of bubbles. The churning water clawed and stabbed at me with its coldness. It twisted me. It spun me over and around. I closed my eyes. And I was too numb to cry out or pray or even think right.

Something heavy hit me.

It was Erik as he tumbled past me.

The water was so spiteful cold it hurt my eyes to open them, but I had to keep sight of Erik. He rolled and bumped along the river bed as the current tossed him about, but I was sure he'd got the picking wire in his hand. The same one that I'd kissed into his mouth. And he was working hard on his padlock.

But now my chest was burning.

I was colder than I'd ever been, yet my chest was on fire – I needed to draw a breath. Bubbles of desperate air slipped out of my mouth and nose. I was faint with cold and fear, but I had to focus. Otherwise I'd forget and gulp for a breath, and all I'd gulp would be a mouthful of freezing river water.

I tried to hold on. I couldn't hold on ...

How long was a second? How long could a burning, painful, terrifying second go on?

Then Erik was in front of me. His chains had gone. He was free. I was so dizzy with my held-in breath it was like a dream. I was so cold I couldn't feel anything. How could he even feel that little picking wire was in his fingers? He jabbed and scratched at the padlock that held my chains.

But I knew he was never going to save me ... I loved him with all my exploding heart for trying. But it was impossible.

I thought death felt light, weightless ...

But it was the heavy chains slipping away.

I thought angels were pulling me towards Heaven ...

But it was Erik dragging me up to the surface.

And the air I found there was amazing. I gasped it down in great, greedy gulps.

CHAPTER 10

The Five-Cent Circus

I want to finish this story by telling you about Erik's first ever performance, but there are loose ends to tie up first.

Jack had made one hell of a hullabaloo when Gus Boydell kidnapped me and Erik. The whole town of Appleton was out looking for us. And when we ended up on the banks of the Fox River, we were spotted right away. We weren't far from where the Boydell brothers had tossed us in, just on the opposite side. Someone wrapped us up in big dry blankets, and hot sweet tea was soon in our hands. My guess is there was a shot of whiskey in the tea too.

Sheriff Cotter led a posse to ride out to find the Boydell brothers. It didn't take long to track them down. And it took even less time to hang them. That's just what was done to those kind of men back in the America of 1885. But I don't want to end Erik's story like that.

How about I tell you that I'm close to being an old lady of fifty now? I have three children, seven grandchildren and I'm the one and only boss of Hanover Hardware. My dear papa passed away in the harsh winter of 1902. I kept the name "Hanover" for our hardware store, even though my own surname is Hoefler now. It's been that way since I married Jack back in 1890.

So that meant Jack never did make it as an acrobat or a magician. I don't think he minds too much. I believe he'd say that we've had a happy life. He'd tell you he may never have become famous, but these days the only shoes he polishes are his own.

Erik, on the other hand, became very famous indeed.

Following our dip in the Fox River, Jack ran out of excuses not to let Erik join his Five-Cent Circus. I reckon the whole town turned up at the park to watch the pair of them perform. After all, the story of how Erik had saved me spread around Appleton faster than nits in a kindergarten. It was a lot of five cents we collected that day. And when I say the whole town, I mean Doc Lansdale, the Dannoy sisters, Sheriff Cotter, even Papa. It was like a public holiday just for our town in that park that day. But all those people just made me more nervous because I had an important part in the performance too.

Jack and Erik read and re-read that book of Robert-Houdin's for inspiration. They'd squabbled and bickered much less than I'd thought they would.

On the day of the Five-Cent Circus, they made a stage out of upturned crates on the grass. Jack changed his name just for the day. He wanted to be known as Jack Roberti in honour of their new hero, and also because he said it sounded more thrilling than plain old Hoefler.

Jack Roberti, King of Tumblers, bent over backwards to pick a pin up with his teeth. He walked his tightrope. But he also performed card tricks and grinned and grinned at the cheers and the applause from the crowd.

But what the crowd really wanted to see was a performance from Erik. He was the boy who could unlock all the shop doors along College Avenue, plus the sheriff's handcuffs and even underwater padlocks.

Erik stepped up onto the wobbly crate stage and held out the heavy chains. They glinted in the sharp autumn sun. Next, he invited a member of the crowd to check them, to prove they were real. Sheriff Cotter stepped forward. Erik had him look over the padlock too.

"You have heard how I use special tools, picking wires, and with them I can unfasten any lock," Erik told the crowd in a loud clear voice. "But today I will use just the power of my mind. My mind will be the magic key that sets me free. Please, Sheriff, could you search me for picking wires, tools or even keys?"

The crowd laughed with delight – they thought it was hilarious to see the sheriff search and pat down the eleven-year-old boy.

"So you agree I have nothing I can use – no keys or special tools?" Erik asked.

The sheriff agreed.

The crowd oohed and aahed.

Erik called for two strong men to wrap him up in the chains and to fasten the hefty heavy padlock. Doc Lansdale and Yardley the butcher were happy to volunteer.

Doc Lansdale yanked the chains so tight that Erik staggered and winced as his breath was squeezed out of him.

"You're going to make a fool of yourself today, boy," Doc Lansdale bellowed.

The crowd booed the old man. They all wanted Erik to amaze them.

"Now I just need one more assistant," Erik said. "Marvellous Mattie, please step up – for it is she who will cover me with a silk sheet while I perform my magical escape."

This was when I stepped onto that make-shift stage, carrying a pure white sheet.

But before I threw it over Erik's head I gave my one line:

"First of all, a kiss for good luck!"

The crowd roared as I planted a huge smacker of a kiss on Erik's lips. I couldn't help but blush. Then I draped the sheet over his head and let it fall all the way to his feet.

I slowly counted to thirty in my head, just as we'd practised – letting the crowd marvel, but also giving Erik plenty of time. Then I whisked the sheet off again.

Erik dropped the chains and padlock from his body and waved his unbound hands in the air. The crowd went wild with cheers.

I looked at Erik and knew that my friend would become very familiar with that sound.

“Thank you,” Erik shouted above the uproar. “Thank you.” He bowed deeply. “Thank you for coming to our Five-Cent Circus.”

Jack joined Erik on stage to take the bows. It was the one and only time they performed together.

“I am Jack Roberti, the King of Tumblers,” Jack shouted.

“And I am Erik Houdini, the King of Escape.”

At that moment Erik was looking out at a crowd of regular Appleton townsfolk, but the shine in his eyes told me he was imagining the vast audiences in cities like New York and London. And perhaps he was already thinking of changing his first name too.

On the very next day, my friend Erik left Appleton for ever.

So I guess the end of this story is really a beginning. I'm proud to have known Erik Weiss and to have been there at his very first performance. I'm proud to have played a part in his amazing story. And, up until this day, I've never told a soul how the trick was done.

THE BEGINNING

Our books are tested
for children and young people by
children and young people.

Thanks to everyone who consulted on
a manuscript for their time and effort in
helping us to make our books better
for our readers.